BLACK COWBOY WILD HORSES

A True Story

JULIUS LESTER ☆ JERRY PINKNEY

Dial Books for Young Readers New York

To Jerry Pinkney

J. L.

To Julius Lester and shared adventures

J. P.

FIRST LIGHT. Bob Lemmons rode his horse slowly up the rise. When he reached the top, he stopped at the edge of the bluff. He looked down at the corral where the other cowboys were beginning the morning chores, then turned away and stared at the land stretching as wide as love in every direction. The sky was curved as if it were a lap on which the earth lay napping like a curled cat. High above, a hawk was suspended on cold threads of unseen winds. Far, far away, at what looked to be the edge of the world, land and sky kissed.

He guided Warrior, his black stallion, slowly down the bluff. When they reached the bottom, the horse reared, eager to run across the vastness of the plains until he reached forever. Bob smiled and patted him gently on the neck. "Easy. Easy," he whispered. "We'll have time for that. But not yet."

He let the horse trot for a while, then slowed him and began peering intently at the ground as if looking for the answer to a question he scarcely understood.

It was late afternoon when he saw them—the hoofprints of mustangs, the wild horses that lived on the plains. He stopped, dismounted, and walked around carefully until he had seen all the prints. Then he got down on his hands and knees to examine them more closely.

Some people learned from books. Bob had been a slave and never learned to read words. But he could look at the ground and read what animals had walked on it, their size and weight, when they had passed by, and where they were going. No one he knew could bring in mustangs by themselves, but Bob could make horses think he was one of them—because he was.

He stood, reached into his saddlebag, took out an apple, and gave it to
Warrior, who chewed with noisy enthusiasm. It was a herd of eight mares, a
colt, and a stallion. They had passed there two days ago. He would see them
soon. But he needed to smell of sun, moon, stars, and wind before the
mustangs would accept him.

The sun went down and the chilly night air came quickly. Bob took the
saddle, saddlebag, and blanket off Warrior. He was cold, but could not make
a fire. The mustangs would smell the smoke in his clothes from miles away.
He draped a thick blanket around himself, then took the cotton sack of dried
fruit, beef jerky, and nuts from his saddlebag and ate. When he was done,
he lay his head on his saddle and was quickly asleep. Warrior grazed in the
tall, sweet grasses.

As soon as the sun's round shoulders came over the horizon, Bob awoke. He ate, filled his canteen, and saddling Warrior, rode away. All day he followed the tracks without hurrying.

Near dusk, clouds appeared, piled atop each other like mountains made of fear. Lightning flickered from within them like candle flames shivering in a breeze. Bob heard the faint but distinct rumbling of thunder. Suddenly lightning vaulted from cloud to cloud across the curved heavens.

Warrior reared, his front hooves pawing as if trying to knock the white streaks of fire from the night sky. Bob raced Warrior to a nearby ravine as the sky exploded sheets of light. And there, in the distance, beneath the ghostly light, Bob saw the herd of mustangs. As if sensing their presence, Warrior rose into the air once again, this time not challenging the heavens but almost in greeting. Bob thought he saw the mustang stallion rise in response as the earth shuddered from the sound of thunder.

Then the rain came as hard and sting-
ing as remorse. Quickly Bob put on his
poncho, and turning Warrior away from
the wind and the rain, waited. The storm
would pass soon. Or it wouldn't. There
was nothing to do but wait.

Finally the rain slowed and then
stopped. The clouds thinned, and there,
high in the sky, the moon appeared as
white as grief. Bob slept in the saddle
while Warrior grazed on the wet grasses.

The sun rose into a clear sky and Bob
was awake immediately. The storm would
have washed away the tracks, but they
had been going toward the big river. He
would go there and wait.

By mid-afternoon he could see the ribbon of river shining in the distance. He stopped, needing only to be close enough to see the horses when they came to drink. Toward evening he saw a trail of rolling, dusty clouds.

In front was the mustang herd. As it reached the water, the stallion slowed and stopped. He looked around, his head raised, nostrils flared, smelling the air. He turned in Bob's direction and sniffed the air again.

Bob tensed. Had he come too close too soon? If the stallion smelled anything new, he and the herd would be gone and Bob would never find them again. The stallion seemed to be looking directly at him. Bob was too far away to be seen, but he did not even blink his eyes, afraid the stallion would hear the sound. Finally the stallion began drinking and the other horses followed. Bob let his breath out slowly. He had been accepted.

The next morning he crossed the river and picked up the herd's trail. He moved Warrior slowly, without sound, without dust. Soon he saw them grazing. He stopped. The horses did not notice him. After a while he moved forward, slowly, quietly. The stallion raised his head. Bob stopped.

When the stallion went back to grazing, Bob moved forward again. All day Bob watched the herd, moving only when it moved but always coming closer. The mustangs sensed his presence. They thought he was a horse. So did he.

The following morning Bob and Warrior walked into the herd. The stallion eyed them for a moment. Then, as if to test this newcomer, he led the herd off in a gallop. Bob lay flat across Warrior's back and moved with the herd. If anyone had been watching, they would not have noticed a man among the horses.

When the herd set out early the next day, it was moving slowly. If the horses had been going faster, it would not have happened.

The colt fell to the ground as if he had stepped into a hole and broken his leg. Bob and the horses heard the chilling sound of the rattles. Rattlesnakes didn't always give a warning before they struck. Sometimes, when someone or something came too close, they bit with the fury of fear.

The horses whinnied and pranced nervously, smelling the snake and death among them. Bob saw the rattler, as beautiful as a necklace, sliding silently through the tall grasses. He made no move to kill it. Everything in nature had the right to protect itself, especially when it was afraid.

The stallion galloped to the colt. He pushed at him. The colt struggled to get up, but fell to his side, shivering and kicking feebly with his thin legs. Quickly he was dead.

Already vultures circled high in the sky. The mustangs milled aimlessly. The colt's mother whinnied, refusing to leave the side of her colt. The stallion wanted to move the herd from there, and pushed the mare with his head. She refused to budge, and he nipped her on the rump. She skittered away. Before she could return to the colt, the stallion bit her again, this time harder. She ran toward the herd. He bit her a third time, and the herd was off. As they galloped away, Bob looked back. The vultures were descending from the sky as gracefully as dusk.

It was time to take over the herd. The stallion would not have the heart to fight fiercely so soon after the death of the colt. Bob galloped Warrior to the front and wheeled around, forcing the stallion to stop quickly. The herd, confused, slowed and stopped also.

Bob raised Warrior to stand high on his back legs, fetlocks pawing and kicking the air. The stallion's eyes widened. He snorted and pawed the ground, surprised and uncertain. Bob charged at the stallion.

Both horses rose on hind legs, teeth bared as they kicked at each other. When they came down, Bob charged Warrior at the stallion again, pushing him backward. Bob rushed yet again.

The stallion neighed loudly, and nipped Warrior on the neck. Warrior snorted angrily, reared, and kicked out with his forelegs, striking the stallion on the nose. Still maintaining his balance, Warrior struck again and again. The mustang stallion cried out in pain. Warrior pushed hard against the stallion. The stallion lost his footing and fell to the earth. Warrior rose, neighing triumphantly, his front legs pawing as if seeking for the rungs on which he could climb a ladder into the sky.

The mustang scrambled to his feet, beaten. He snorted weakly. When Warrior made as if to attack again, the stallion turned, whinnied weakly, and trotted away.

Bob was now the herd's leader, but would they follow him? He rode slowly at first, then faster and faster. The mustangs followed as if being led on ropes. Throughout that day and the next he rode with the horses. For Bob there was only the bulging of the horses' dark eyes, the quivering of their flesh, the rippling of muscles and bending of bones in their bodies. He was now sky and plains and grass and river and horse.

When his food was almost gone, Bob led the horses on one last ride, a dark surge of flesh flashing across the plains like black lightning. Toward evening he led the herd up the steep hillside, onto the bluff, and down the slope toward the big corral. The cowboys heard him coming and opened the corral gate. Bob led the herd, but at the last moment he swerved Warrior aside, and the mustangs flowed into the fenced enclosure. The cowboys leaped and shouted as they quickly closed the gate.

Bob rode away from them and back up to the bluff. He stopped and
stared out onto the plains. Warrior reared and whinnied loudly.
"I know," Bob whispered. "I know. Maybe someday."
Maybe someday they would ride with the mustangs,
ride to that forever place where land and sky kissed,
and then
ride on.
Maybe someday.

This is a true story based on the life of a black cowboy named Bob Lemmons. He is mentioned in two books: *The Adventures of the Negro Cowboys* by Philip Durham and *The Mustangs* by Everett L. Jones and J. Frank Dobie. In the latter there is an interview with Lemmons when he was in his eighties. I told this story first in my book *Long Journey Home: Stories from Black History* (Dial Books, 1972, reissued 1993). The present version was inspired by a fascination with black cowboys that Jerry Pinkney and I discovered we share. Jerry sent me a copy of a 1975 calendar he illustrated depicting blacks in the West and said he would love to do a book about black cowboys. I sent him a copy of *Long Journey Home* and asked him to read "The Man Who Was a Horse." He read it and said he would love to illustrate it, but thought it would be very difficult to rewrite the story as a picture book. I didn't tell him that I thought the *real* hard work was going to be the illustrations. May we each keep believing that our job is the easier one.

J. L.

As a young boy growing up in Philadelphia, PA, I dreamed of exploring the Wild West. My friends and I played cowboys, and with great enthusiasm we became characters portrayed on the silver screen. What fun we had. Today I wonder how our role-playing and self-esteem would have been enhanced had we known about Nat Love, the black cowboy, Bill Pickett, the black rodeo star, and the fact that one out of three cowboys was black or Mexican.

Some thirty years later I got my chance to play cowboys again, with a project I created for an African-American history calendar. The subject was the Black West, and it was that calendar I shared with Julius Lester. So again, some twenty-two years later I am playing cowboys. This time I am illustrating the story of Bob Lemmons, herding wild horses on the western plains. My gear is the finely crafted text written by Julius and my ever increasing appetite for American history. It is also the mounting research on this nation's true West, with—of course—cowboys of color.

J. P.

Published by Dial Books for Young Readers
A division of Penguin Young Readers Group
345 Hudson Street • New York, New York 10014

Text copyright © 1998 by Julius Lester
Pictures copyright © 1998 by Jerry Pinkney
All rights reserved • Designed by Atha Tehon
Manufactured in China on acid-free paper
10
Library of Congress Cataloging in Publication Data

Lester, Julius.
Black cowboy, wild horses : a true story / by Julius Lester ; pictures by Jerry Pinkney. — 1st ed.
p. cm.
Summary: A black cowboy is so in tune with wild mustangs that they accept him into the herd,
thus enabling him singlehandedly to take them to the corral.
ISBN 0-8037-1787-3 (trade). — ISBN 0-8037-1788-1 (lib)
[1. Mustang — Fiction. 2. Horses — Fiction. 3. Cowboys — Fiction.
4. Afro-Americans — Fiction.] I. Pinkney, Jerry, ill. II. Title.
PZ7.L5629Man 1998 [E]—DC21 97-25210 CIP AC

The full-color artwork was prepared using pencil, gouache, and watercolor on paper.